For Markel Harris
—M.B.

For Grams, whose stories are mostly magic
—E.P.

THE MAGIC WORD

Written by **Mac Barnett**   Illustrated by **Elise Parsley**

BALZER + BRAY
An Imprint of HarperCollinsPublishers

On Friday night at 8:45, Paxton C. Heymeyer of 23 Larch Street asked for a cookie.

The babysitter said, "What's the magic word?"

It's hard to say why Paxton did what he did.
Maybe he thought it would be funny. Maybe he
didn't like the way the babysitter was smiling at
him. Or maybe he was tired of adults asking him
to say the magic word.

But instead of saying "Can I have a cookie, *please*?"
Paxton C. Heymeyer said, "Can I have a cookie,

ALAKAZOOMBA?"

There was a puff of blue smoke,
and a cookie appeared in his hand.

The babysitter stared. "Give me that cookie."

"Why?" Paxton asked.

"Because you didn't say the magic word."

"I think I did," said Paxton.

Then Paxton scratched his ear and said, "Can I have another cookie,

"And some milk, **ALAKAZOOMBA**."

The babysitter scowled. "Paxton C. Heymeyer, put those cookies back in the jar. Pour that milk back in the carton. You have until the count of three."

"One," said the babysitter.

"Two," said the babysitter.

"Can I have a walrus that will chase the babysitter up to the North Pole, **ALAKAZOOMBA**?" said Paxton.

And he got one.

That's how Paxton C. Heymeyer discovered the magic word.

At half past nine Paxton's parents returned and found 23 Larch looked a bit different.

"Paxton C. Heymeyer, get down here right now!" said Mrs. H.

Paxton slid down the waterslide into the living room. "Do you like what I've done with the place?"

"You?" said his father. "You did all this?"

"Yeah!" said Paxton. "Will you tuck me into bed?"

"Paxton," said his mother, "you are grounded."

Well, that wasn't good. "Could I get another one of those walruses, **ALAKAZOOMBA**?"

That night Paxton ate cookies in bed.

The next morning he got right to work.

At lunchtime, the new robot chef brought Paxton some cookies. "I bet Rosie would get a kick out of this," Paxton said.

At a quarter to four, Rosie knocked at the door and was let in by the butler.

"What's with the elephant?" asked Rosie.

"You mean Angelo?" said Paxton. "He's my new pet."

"How'd you get him?" Rosie asked.

Paxton told her about the magic word. "You mean," said Rosie, "you could have anything in the world, and this is what you asked for?"

"Want to go hang gliding?" asked Paxton.

"No," said Rosie.

"I have a shark tank," said Paxton.

"No thanks."

"Let's see all my sneakers!" said Paxton.

"I just wanted to play Go Fish."

"Oh!" said Paxton. "This is just great.
Angelo is a Go Fish–playing elephant!"

"I don't know," said Rosie, "this elephant isn't very much *fun* to play cards with."

"Hmm," said Paxton. "You could let the robot play your hand, and we could just watch."

"That's boring," said Rosie.

"Sneaker time!" said Paxton.

"Pax," said Rosie, "you're a terrible host."

Well, Paxton wasn't going to stand there and be insulted in his very own house, let alone his very own castle with a helipad and pink-lemonade moat.

"WALRUS, ALAKAZOOMBA."

ALAKAZOOMBA.

Who needed Rosie?
Paxton could do whatever he wanted.

That was great, right?

ALAKAZOOMBA.

That night, Paxton couldn't get to sleep.

The chef wheeled over. "Another cookie, Young Master Heymeyer?"

"No thanks," Paxton said.

He turned in his bed, and his sheets all came loose. The butler was no good at tucking him in.

He flipped on the lights. "Angelo!"

Rosie was right about one thing. The elephant wasn't much fun to play cards with.

At midnight Paxton made up his mind. "All right, walruses. Bring everyone back, **ALAKAZOOMBA**."

Paxton coughed. Here came the hard part.

"Sorry, Mom. Sorry, Dad."

His parents gave him a kiss.

"Sorry, Rosie," said Paxton.

"Humph," said Rosie.

"No, really," said Paxton.

"Yeah, right," said Rosie.

"FORGIVE ME, ALAKAZOOMBA!"

"There's no magic word, Pax. You just have to mean it."

Paxton put his hands in his pockets. "But I do. I am sorry."

"Good!" Rosie said. "I forgive you."

He turned to his babysitter.

"Don't even bother," she said. "If you think for one second that I will ever, EVER, forgive a spoiled little—"

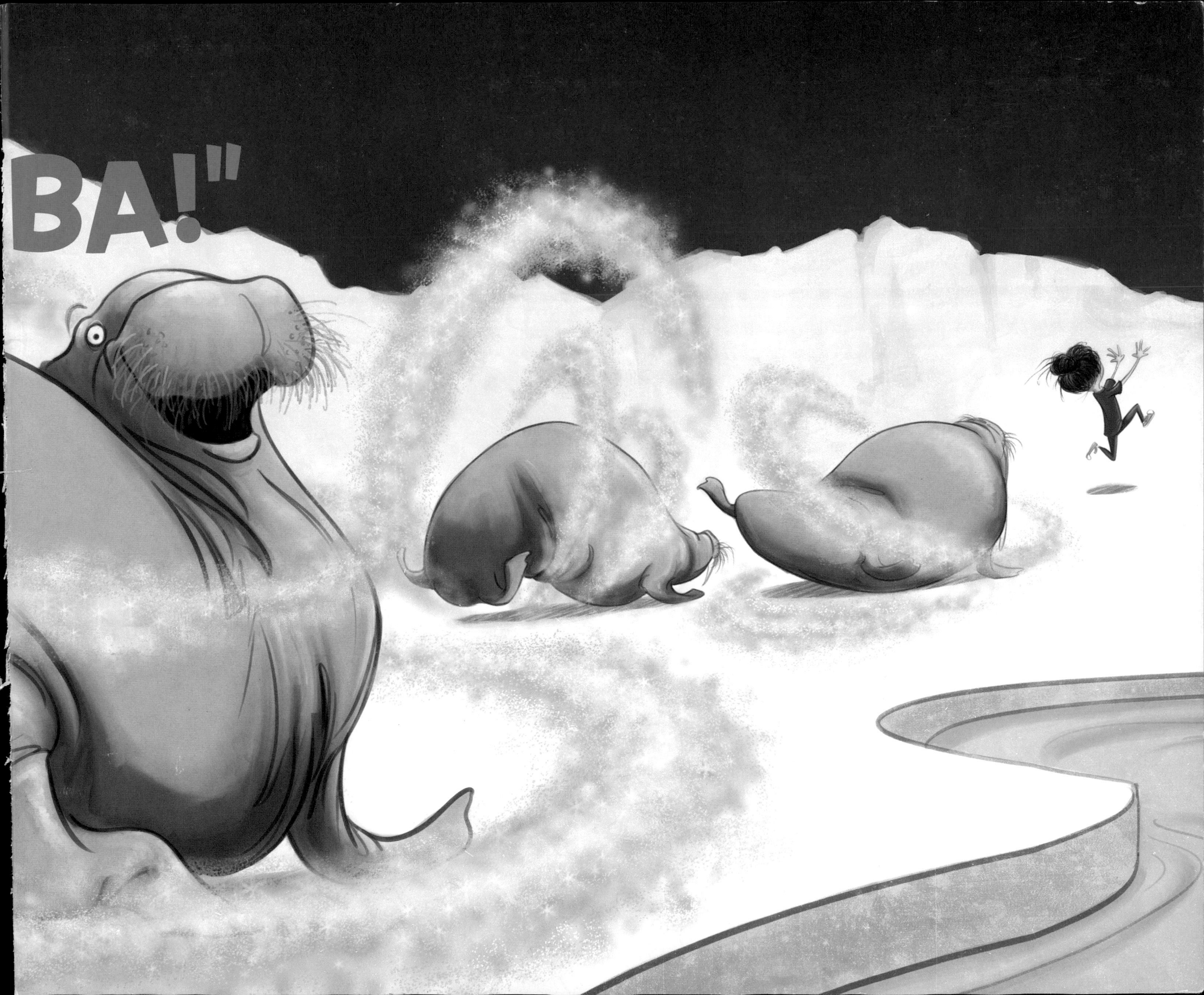
BA!"

Balzer + Bray is an imprint of HarperCollins Publishers.
The Magic Word
Text copyright © 2016 by Mac Barnett
Illustrations copyright © 2016 by Elise Parsley

Library of Congress Control Number: 2015947613
ISBN 978-0-06-235484-6

The artist digitally drew the illustrations for this book in Adobe Photoshop and digitally painted them
in Corel Painter using a Monoprice Tablet.
Typography by Dana Fritts
16 17 18 19 20 SCP 10 9 8 7 6 5 4 3 2 1
❖ First Edition